To Bna

Friend, poet —
I hope to collaborate
for years to come. ..

Thank you!

2014

PURE SLUSH BOOKS

praise for
*The Vixen Scream
and other Bible Stories*

Hilarious, irreverent, twisted, bawdy, brilliant – these short shorts by Nancy Stohlman feel like a series of off-kilter encounters with the strangest characters you swear you've met before in a previous, more interesting lifetime. With sly humor and daring, Stohlman weaves tiny tales reminiscent of Etgar Keret, but with her own inimitable stamp. *The Vixen Scream and other Bible Stories* is an amazing collection. Do not deny yourself the pleasure of reading it.

– Kathy Fish, author of *Together We Can Bury It*

The Vixen Scream is a collection of compelling and strikingly original stories – an imagination functioning at full throttle. Nancy Stohlman is a word-alchemist, and here is her book of wonders!

– Robert Scotellaro, author of *Measuring the Distance*

Nancy Stohlman's *The Vixen Scream* is warped and wonderful, a sometimes poignant, sometimes hilarious flash fiction romp. I thoroughly enjoyed this book, never sure what I'd encounter on the next page but knowing I'd always be entertained – and more often than not, delighted.

– Tom Hazuka, author of *Flash Fiction*, *Flash Fiction Funny*, *Sudden Flash Youth*, and *You Have Time For This*

Nancy Stohlman wrings epiphanies and hallelujahs from the flash fiction miracles in *The Vixen Scream and other Bible Stories*. Stohlman is the Patron Saint of Flash Fiction and the Pirate Queen of Inventiveness. She infuses her stories with a richness of language, a depth of the surreal, and a healthy infusion of sanguine wit, guaranteeing readers fall at her feet in worship.

– James Claffey, author of *Blood A Cold Blue*

Stohlman conjures up haunting blasts of wild-skewered, hilarious, subversive worlds within her masterful hands. *The Vixen Scream and other Bible Stories* is an original collection of flash beauties, peopled by "still-warm keys, propping the lid, listening to her heart." Stohlman is inimitable and unforgettable! Get a copy!

– Meg Tuite, author of *Bound By Blue*

Blasphemously funny and potent. Sudden fiction doesn't get any foxier than this.

– Christopher Allen, author of *Conversations with S. Teri O'Type (a Satire)*

In *The Vixen Scream*, Nancy Stohlman handles tiny men, death row inmates, pops, Avon lady stalkers, missing penises, clones with bad taste in literature, and a shitload of Biblical characters. This is a fun, profound, and brilliant world of eclectic stories that will have you laughing as you wonder, "Why didn't I come up with this?" Somehow, Stohlman expertly creates vivid worlds in tiny stories that leap off the page and into the dark places of your soul.

– Nathaniel Tower, author of *Nagging Wives, Foolish Husbands*, and Managing Editor of *Bartleby Snopes Literary Magazine*

also by Nancy Stohlman

novels

The Monster Opera

Searching for Suzi: a flash novel

anthologies

Fast Forward: The Mix Tape (ed.)

Live From Palestine (ed.)

Fast Forward: An Anthology of Flash Fiction Vol 1 (ed.)

Fast Forward: An Anthology of Flash Fiction Vol 2 (ed.)

The
Vixen
Scream
and other
Bible Stories

Nancy Stohlman

a Pure Slush book

First published October 2014

Copyright © Nancy Stohlman

Pure Slush Books
4 Warburton Street
Magill SA 5072
Australia
Email: edpureslush@live.com.au
Website: http://pureslush.webs.com
Visit the Pure Slush Store: http://pureslush.webs.com/store.htm

Front cover photograph copyright © Nancy Stohlman
Author photograph copyright © Lynn Hough / And Everything Else Photography

ISBN: 978-1-925101-11-9

for my fox

Contents

Death Row Hugger

For some reason it's always at night. It's always the same room, the light's always jaundiced. The room smells musty, like wet clothes were shoved and left to die in all the corners.

I guess I was destined for this job. My parents weren't the hugging type, so I've always had a malnourished craving for arms around me. I started as a professional baby cuddler for preemies in the NICU; each night after visiting hours, I settled into a wooden rocking chair with these miniature babies and their ancient faces and whispered of a future when they'd be strong and full-sized.

But nothing could prepare me for being a Volunteer Hugger on Death Row. You enter that holding room, and there they are, trying to enjoy their steaks or lobsters or Cuban cigars or whatever. My job is to hug them just before they take that long walk. It's not a sexual hug, though I have felt a few erections, and a few have tried to kiss me, but I politely turn my cheek and squeeze them harder. Because there's this moment in the hug, you see, where it goes from something awkward and obligatory to when they melt into my arms, weeping with their bodies. Every now and then I hear one whisper in my ear, and once one called me Mama.

The Homunculus

After all my other birthday presents were opened, he had one last gift for me. It was a tiny box he held out with such a grin that I became nervous. What is it? I asked. Just open it, he said. Inside was a tiny man, about 6 inches high. He was dressed in tiny Polo jeans and a tiny madras shirt with pullover sweater, and he looked very much like a tiny version of my boyfriend.

It's a homunculus, he said. Since I have to be out of town so much for work, and I know how much you hate being alone, this will be the perfect solution! It'll be like we're together all the time.

But how will I take care of him?

He's a grown man, he can take care of himself.

It was a bit awkward at first, but my boyfriend reassured me it would be fine. So I put him in the inside pocket of my purse, where I keep special things like my mirror and my flash drive. He never complained, even when I once saw him all twisted under some lipsticks and dirty from the random filth that collects at the bottom of purses.

I felt bad, so I started taking him out more often. He got brave enough to sit at the edge of my plate and eat with me; I didn't have tiny utensils, so he used his hands. He was always clean, even though he wore the same clothes, all the time. When I asked him about it, he just said, I'm a homunculus.

We were really hitting it off, which shouldn't be surprising. He was just like my boyfriend—except tinier. And more available. We liked all the same things. I started taking him out of my purse when watching a movie, sitting in front of the fireplace; I put him in my breast pocket on bike rides, and eventually I let him sleep on the pillow next to me. The first night I was terrified I would roll over him, but he was fine in the morning and I started to relax, and then on one of those mornings I let him go beneath my panties when we were lying there, and things happened.

That's when I started to feel guilty—what would my boyfriend think? The more time that passed the more I rationalized. But I didn't want to admit the truth—I was falling for the little guy.

The first night my boyfriend got back into town was strange—it felt weird to sleep next to a full-sized person again, and I lay awake for the longest night of my life, worried about the homunculus, who was back in my purse.

The next morning after my boyfriend had left, the homunculus climbed up the mattress and found me on the pillows. Let's run away, I suggested. I couldn't stand the thought of not being with him. Then I heard my boyfriend coming up the stairs. He arrived in the doorway as I tried to hide the homunculus. But he must have seen it in my eyes, because he yanked the pillow away and there was the homunculus, trying to disappear between the folds of the comforter.

You backstabber! he yelled, snatching him and running down the stairs. I followed, screaming—don't hurt him! For god's sake, you're crushing him!

My boyfriend ran out the front door and across the street and all the way to the top of Jackass Hill, where he wound up his arm and threw my homunculus as far as he could. I saw his tiny dot fly through the air until he disappeared into the blue sky.

Almost Pope

Outside the smoke billows black while inside everyone waits. I'm in the dressing room, applying more lipstick. The other contestants for Pope are pacing, praying, primping. Everyone here wants the same thing. I already rocked the evening gown and talent portions, but he did kill it on the interview question.

Now he and I are standing next to each other and the crowd is ravenous and the MC is explaining how important the first runner-up is because if anything happens and the Pope can't finish out his term, then the first runner-up will become Pope—and now he and I are squeezing hands, and I'm praying and he's praying...

When they call my name as the first runner-up I'm not sure whether to scream or cry. The new Pope turns to me bawling and jumping and we're hugging and the old Pope is bringing over the gold cape and the big Pope hat. On all the teleprompters the smoke outside the building turns white.

The Fox

I first saw him on the dirt bike path behind the Lightrail. He was 50 yards away, scratching in the warm spring sun, reddish brown coat, black paws, white belly. I stood very still, and when he didn't run I took a soft step, wondering how close I could get. He preened until I was quite close; his nose was long and sweet. And then, when I was just 10 feet away, he excused himself into the bushes with calculated nonchalance, a final flick of his white-tipped tail.

I walked the rest of the way home feeling exquisite.

Later on my porch, in the temptations of dusk, I sensed him before I saw him, emerging from the overgrowth and into the din of the streetlights. He had the curious look of a boy, new and fresh and wild and sensuous, with vulnerable brown eyes.

I thought about leaving food but I was afraid the squirrels would get it. So instead I left my pillow— covered in the smells of me at my most peaceful and innocent. An invitation. That night he entered my dreams and I embraced a coarse lean body, strong wiry legs wrapped around my waist in an almost human way.

In the morning the pillow had been nested in, a few scattered white hairs left in the circular impression of his body. I held it to my nose and inhaled the musky, wild smell.

Each night I left the pillow on my porch and each night he returned, inching it closer to the front door until the night I left the door open. The moon cast a square beam onto the living room floor, and there I lay, almost sick with nerves, when I felt bristles of fur tickle the edge of the sheet. His nose brushed my toe, touched my hair. I held my breath. He circled a few times, gently trampling down the bedding, then settled behind me, his face tucked into the crook of my neck.

The wind blew through the open door and smoothed our entwined faces. I surrendered to sleep in the hazy, bird-chirpy morning, and when I awoke he was gone.

But I found his gift left lovingly for me on the pillow: my black cat, lifeless. I felt strangely unmoved as I sniffed it, nudged it with my nose.

Lazarus

After three days in a cold, silent tomb, Lazarus was resurrected from the dead in a miracle to surpass all miracles: women fainted, men fell to their knees and became instant believers, and even disbelievers paused before they claimed it was trickery from the devil.

Now Lazarus sat wrapped in a blanket, watching Jesus leave for Jerusalem with his entourage. He was still wearing his burial robes, full of the smell of his own decay. His eyes hurt from the sun. The townspeople were watching him from an awkward distance, a series of pregnant pauses like dots on the horizon.

A woman finally came forward. "Do you want some water or something?"

He looked back at the open tomb and shook his head.

I'm Being Stalked by the Avon Lady

At first it wasn't so bad. She'd show up in her pencil skirts and French manicures and support hose and I just thought it was good customer service. But soon I started noticing little extras inside the plastic bags, weird hearts drawn next to her phone number, and then one morning I caught her peeking in my front windows when I didn't have to be at work early. When I said "What are you doing?" she blushed and tried to hand me this month's Birthstone Bracelet. It was green—August. I'm sure I'd never told her my birthday.

The next week she was back, delivering wrinkle creams in white paper bags. She rang my doorbell even though I hadn't ordered anything. I stood on the other side of the screen suspiciously. I wanted to give you some samples of our new bath elixir bulbs, she said. Please. I cracked the door enough to grab one. You just put them in the bath and they are so fantastic. But her voice was shaky on the word fantastic and inside the bag was a note: Help me.

I thought about calling Avon Customer Service but I decided to follow her instead. She unlocked a normal looking two-story home and I saw a little basement window turn on. I got close enough to see the floor piled with undelivered books and empty plastic baggies. I could hear muffled screaming and then a glass tube splattered against the wall, its contents oozed to the floor.

I went back after dark and positioned myself again by the tiny window; I tapped softly on the glass and she came, wearing the latest shade of Sassy Tangerine lipstick. Take this she said, passing me a pair of 14 k Metallic Sweetheart earrings on sale this month only. Hurry, they'll be back soon she said, pushing the earrings through the bars.

The next day I saw her in the neighborhood delivering Avon books out of a little red wagon in her faux leopard print pumps. She was wearing sunglasses, a dark spot on her chin that had been shabbily concealed with the new Daywear Delight All Day Foundation. I found myself hating her, hating all her stupid lipstick samples and her childish gullibility.

The next week there was a new lady, a bright-smiled woman wearing a fuchsia two-piece suit and last season's Whimsical Woods body fragrance. What happened to the other one? I asked. She didn't work out the new Avon lady answered.

I Pawned My Boyfriend for $85

I'm not saying I'm proud of how it all went down. But maybe if those collection agencies hadn't been calling me all the time. After avoiding another 800 number last Saturday morning, I looked over at you sleeping, lips pursed, eyelids fluttering, all mussed up like a baby koala, and I thought: there are plenty of people out there who would pay good money for that.

You're still pissed. I tried to explain that I won't have the money to get you out until my next paycheck, but the pawnshop owner said that I was just riling up the merchandise and if I wasn't gonna buy nothing then it was time for me to leave.

When I went in today you'd been moved to the front window display wearing a lovely tiara. I wondered if they would give me a deal on both because I really liked that tiara. You looked away when I walked in but then the owner said to be nice to the customers because Father's Day is coming up, after all.

Today is actually our anniversary, but you didn't want to hear it and wouldn't open the card I brought. Look, you can't hold onto your resentment forever I said. But you just turned away, tiara sparkling in the mid-afternoon sun.

The Hole

One day Mr. G started digging a hole. The sound of the shovel hitting dirt over and over prompted the expected neighborhood jokes. But after a few days the hole was much too large to be a grave.

He dug all day, every day, and sometimes he dug into the night, until the neighbors with babies trying to sleep would be forced to cover their pajamas with coats and go ask him to stop. By sunrise he would be digging again.

When it rained he would scoop out bucketsful of mud that dried into large, dung-shaped hills and cracked open in the sun. Sometimes his wife would be out there too, and soon the hole tunneled under the house and you couldn't hear the sounds of the digging anymore, but once or twice a week a friend would be recruited and you'd see them helping lower things into the hole: a couch, a dresser, a washer and dryer. The lawn became increasingly full of desks, dining room sets, televisions, department store-sized racks of clothing, patio furniture.

Slowly each day the hole under the house swallowed these items, until the house and lawn were empty, only a for-sale sign and the faint marks of where things had briefly sat.

Fox II: The Quickening

All the signs were there: engorged breasts, swollen toes, a yeasty fullness in my distended belly. Each morning I doubled over the toilet, vomiting thin yellow bile and tiny mouse carcasses.

At night, while my boyfriend slept, I tiptoed to the window and raised the blinds. My fox would circle, land on a rock. Flick his tail. Bark.

Soon I was sleeping all day, waking at dusk to watch rabbits from the shadows. My fox came every evening and touched his velvet nose to the screen. He coaxed me to the top of Jackass Hill and showed me his favorite place to dig. He brought me to his den by the train tracks but I was too big to fit all the way inside, so we huddled together in the entrance, his bushy tail tucked over my legs.

I returned to Jackass Hill every night, snuck out of my house after dark and slept curled with him until the birds began to stir in the gray sky morning and I returned home, covered in the smells of musk and earth.

Pretty soon it became impossible to hide—little arms and legs clawing to escape, little bodies swelling inside my stomach until it wanted to rip open. One night in late summer I fell to the kitchen floor moaning: out came three tiny babies, matted fur, long wet tails, oversized ears. I lay panting on the tile as they tumbled out, shook off their birth, and ran out the open front door.

I didn't mean to let them go, I cried while my fox circled, helplessly.

The Annunciation

The angel Gabriel appeared at the window. Mary was blinded by the brightness of the light in her face.

Hail Mary, full of grace! the angel said. Do not be afraid: You have been chosen by God to bear his only son. And this son you will call Jesus, and he will be the lamb of the world who will sacrifice himself to save mankind! Hail Mary, blessed are you among women and blessed is the fruit of your womb!

The angel left, and all was quiet again, only the dust particles swirling.

Oh shit, Mary whispered in the dark.

The Mermaid

She was at the billiards hall, playing video poker at the bar. I could tell she was a mermaid right away, something about the silvery sheen of her skin or the way her hair tangled like blond seaweed.

You look familiar I said as I sat down. Do we know each other?

She rolled her eyes and avoided my gaze, slammed a bright blue drink and muttered something about I'm not from here.

But when I heard her salty voice, I knew. I'd been sitting on the crags off the coast of France, watching the waves crash blue and white foam against dark brown rocks. The Sirens were clustered just out of reach, past the break, their heads bobbing with the moving sea. An old crabber yelled *Stop!* as I threw myself into the swirling waters, kicking against the current. They were floating with the waves, watching me approach. They lowered their eyelids and puckered strawberry lips at me, and each time I was within reach she would slip away until finally I managed to seize one, a mass of slippery vanilla skin. She thrashed like a beautiful trout as I dragged her back to the shore; her scales drew blood as she flailed and cried, a piercing sound that hurt my ears, and the old crabber watched me in disbelief, and the closer we got to the shore the more limp and heavy she became until she surrendered completely. I dragged her through the pebbly shallows and laid her at the edge of the water where her tail would stay wet. She curled away from me and avoided my gaze, much as she was doing now. Her gills moved slowly, beautiful and doomed, as the horizon swallowed the sun and the sea became a sound only.

You were the one in France, I finally said.

I'm not a mermaid anymore, in case you're wondering, she answered, and then she ordered another shot and turned her stool away.

My House is in the Contemporary Art Museum

Let me clarify: I don't technically live *in* the museum, but my front door is between the bathrooms and the elevator. I was warned about the unusual situation when I first looked at the place—chic, lots of square footage for the money, this museum thing being the only downside, though it does come with a free membership and a stack of guest passes. And it's only the entering and leaving that's an issue, especially if I have two armloads of groceries and I'm digging for my keys next to the new Pop Art exhibit. But on Mondays when the museum is closed, it's just like living anywhere.

I looked at other places. I really liked the 75th floor penthouse suite with outdoor hot tub—it had panoramic windows and coin-operated binoculars and a radio tower that blinked a warning for low-flying airplanes. But when the wind blew, the hot tub sloshed and spilled. What's up with the splashing? I asked the realtor, as the apartment swayed in the wind. All things being equal, I just can't deal with a leaky roof.

Then you'll love this next place, the realtor said. It's an artist loft, and check out this view: I followed his gaze downward and through the thick glass floor to the streets below, dotted with lights and taxis and the tiny bustle of umbrellas. Nowhere are you going to find a view like this one. And the glass is completely bulletproof. Well yes, I said, looking longingly between my shoes, but the switching of the traffic lights, yellow, red, green—it's going to keep me up all night.

Then he took me to a three-story antebellum mansion with a swooping circular driveway. It's too big, I said. I just can't imagine myself even having a reason to go upstairs. Well, that's why it might be the perfect fit, he said, because the upper two floors are haunted, so I wouldn't go up there, and the basement's iffy too, so the liveable square footage is only about 1000 feet on the first floor, perfect for a single fellow like yourself. He made a good point, and I told him so. But I'm just not ready for roommates again, I finally said.

I understand, the realtor said. Things are trickier these days, what with all the excessive choices in wind chimes.

I can't be responsible for my lack of wind chimes anymore, I confessed.

Well, the realtor said, I was saving it for last, but I think it's time. And he brought me through the dwindling museum crowds, down the elevator to the lower floor, and around a partition lined with plants. Don't worry, they're fake, he said, seeing my concern. The intercom was announcing 15 minutes until closing in a female voice I would eventually come to love as the realtor unlocked the front door and I glanced at the nameplate. You won't have to do anything out of the ordinary but you will have to be home by 7 pm every night except First Fridays. I'll take it, I said, knowing a good deal when I saw one. Guaranteed not to depreciate, the realtor added. I would have snatched it up myself if it weren't for the wife. He tapped the nameplate with his pencil. The last owner was quite happy here but then he got married.

Now on Sundays I take a café au lait in the gift shop in my robe while reading the *New York Times*. I don't really mind the people, all dressed up, gaping at the Warhols, the Hoppers or the Klees—we smile and acknowledge each other as they wait in line for the elevator and I fumble for my house key.

The Detritus

She feared her husband's death. Though perfectly healthy now, he was sixteen years her senior and simple math made it apparent he was going to leave her well before she was ready. The idea was so terrifying that she secretly wished to die first. "When I die, will you name a park bench after me?" she would ask on random occasions, or, "If I die first, will you marry again?" And he would look at her gently and say, "Baby, when you die, I'll already be long gone."

She became so obsessed with this preordained tragedy and the dreaded, empty future without him that she began to secretly collect pieces of him: silvery hairs left tangled in the sheets, bits of skin left as dust on the mantle, crusted toothpaste scraped from the toothbrush, remnants of wadded up toilet paper from the garbage, stubble wiped from the razor. Each year her collection grew larger.

On the day it happened she was ready; using the surfeit of collected pieces from her dead husband she immediately constructed him again. In this way she was able to avoid even a single morning of the terror she had feared.

Her new husband was identical to the old; he fit so perfectly into the space left behind that she soon forgot there had ever been a breech. He came with all the idiosyncrasies of the other, all the habits good and bad.

They were so identical, in fact, she began to wonder: Could I alter just a few tiny things? It would be just as easy to make him throw his yogurt containers in the garbage, for instance. Soon her new husband was doing things he'd never done in real life—not falling asleep with all the lights on, spooning with her all night long, brushing out her hair, reading side by side with her in bed, vacuuming the stairs, ignoring his collection of spaghetti westerns. He was perfect, she thought one morning while he frothed a perfect cappuccino with perfect poached eggs. It was only then that the loneliness she'd been avoiding finally found her.

Fox III: Jackass Hill

I waited on Jackass Hill as the city faded into dusk. Finally he appeared, the white tip of his bushy tail reflecting the last of the light.

Hi, I said. I wasn't sure if you would come.

He was agitated, pacing, circling. He stopped near my feet, channeled his awkwardness into digging something. He looked thinner, and sadder.

I didn't know if you'd still want to see me.

He stopped digging. Dirt covered his nose. The smile of his spongy black lips against the white fur muzzle was deceiving.

My boyfriend asked me to marry him, I said.

We stared, frozen, until a rock landed between us. Four boys on bicycles approached and he bolted.

Bronzed Heart

After we broke up I didn't know what do with your heart. I tried to give it back but by then you weren't answering your phone. I couldn't throw it away but I also couldn't have it beating like this all the time. So I did the only logical thing: I had it bronzed.

It wasn't as heavy as I thought it might be, and I cleared away a spot on the mantle. It was really lovely, captured in mid-beat, glittering in the morning sunlight. A scientific marvel, the way it tapered at the tip. I read once that your heart was the same size as your fist. I wondered if I threw it at the door if it would make the same-sized hole.

But pretty soon I felt I couldn't keep it on the mantle either because I was trying to date and it was creating too many questions, so I put it in a box at the back of my closet and covered it with winter coats.

Reluctantly I took it to one of those places where they buy gold and silver. The jeweler pulled out a velvet cushion and examined it with a pair of magnifying glasses. It's broken, he said. That's part of its charm, I said. Most people come in here looking for ones that aren't broken. Yes, but look at that magnificent specimen, I said, stroking the muscle and the hint of strong veins. He offered me an amount far higher than I expected, which means it was probably worth more.

You called that day, first time in months. *I feel a big hole like a piece of me is missing,* you said on my answering machine. I didn't call back because I knew you'd hear it in my voice. Just for the hell of it I walked by the gold shop the next day to see how much he'd raised the price and realized I could never afford to get it back.

Indentured

How much are you getting paid to do this? he asks, a crease in his forehead.

Enough to pay off my student loans I said, as he begins to tattoo the Coca-Cola logo across my face.

The Hostess

After the argument the hostess threw a small dinner party, just the neighbors and a few friends, just something to lift her spirits. She made pot roasts and French Onion soup from scratch while he retreated to the basement.

There was a few weeks truce, an uneasy truce for the sake of the children, and then another all-night battle followed by a series of murder mystery parties, complete with costumes, wine tastings, realistic weapons rented by the hour, and yucca whipped into hills as light and fluffy as French pastries.

By the end-of-summer-Hawaiian-luau, the hostess was holding back tears through her fake eyelashes and long, black wig as he moved his things into the spare bedroom: *You invited them, you entertain them!* he yelled, slamming the door. The guests tried to keep her glass filled with an assortment of specialty rums and freshly crushed papaya mixers.

Soon the invitations started going unanswered; the guests found excuses for not attending the 1950's sock hop, the M*A*S*H party, the "1001 Arabian Nights" celebration complete with whole roasted goat. Come spring, the 25-foot-tall Maypole looked desolate, pastel ribbons hanging limply like unwashed hair.

But today, the sound of hammers. It would be the greatest party she had ever thrown. Everyone would come. A crew of a dozen was sawing, hammering, painting, and creating a to-scale facsimile of the Titanic. Another crew was bringing in 500-gallon tanks of water that would, at the appropriate moment, be released into the back yard, while the guests, in turn-of-the-century formalwear (as specified in their invitation) would get into actual lifeboats and attempt to row themselves to the safety of the house. A caterer was reconstructing an iceberg two stories high, and, at 11:40 pm, the gong she rented would sound, the string orchestra would begin to play, the water would begin rise and the guests would file into lifeboats, of which there would, of course, be too few.

Fox IV: The Deluge

At first it was only a hesitant patter—all night and into that lonely morning the rain melted the chalk drawings, saturated the flowerbeds, bruised the tomatoes. People spoke of it in soothing tones, redemption for an exhausted July.

But the rains wouldn't stop. Basements flooded, intersections slipped underwater. Then the strange deaths, people were crushed by crumbling houses, people became waterlogged. Nobody's pants fit right. Skylights shattered. People made makeshift canoes out of flipped bathtubs and convertible tops.

I wonder what the animals do in this weather, my boyfriend said when he caught me staring out the window.

I've never thought about it, I lied.

The Flood

They came in twos: the lions, the giraffes, the elephants, the wolves, a duet of doves, a shrewdness of apes, a business of ferrets, a charm of finches, an exaltation of larks, a shiver of sharks, an unkindness of ravens, a parliament of owls, a descent of woodpeckers, an obstinacy of buffalo, a glaring of cats, a troubling of goldfish, an ostentation of peacocks, a quiver of cobras, a husk of jackrabbits, a watch of nightingales, a stubbornness of rhinoceros, a knot of snakes, a lamentation of swans, a pair of lovebirds cooing promises in the rain, and a single red fox, shaking the gathering drops from its matted face.

Canidae

Arctic fox, *Vulpes lagopus*
Bengal fox, *Vulpes bengalensis*
Blanford's fox, *Vulpes cana*
Cape fox, *Vulpes chama*
Corsac fox, *Vulpes corsac*
Fennec fox, *Vulpes zerda*
Kit fox, *Vulpes macrotis*
Pale fox, *Vulpes pallida*
Rüppell's fox, *Vulpes rueppellii*
Red fox, *Vulpes vulpes* (includes silver fox)
Swift fox, *Vulpes velox*
Tibetan sand fox, *Vulpes ferrilata*

Vulpes Vulpes

The **red fox** (*vulpes vulpes*) is the largest of the true foxes. It is well known for its bushy tail and its ability to adapt to new environments.

Red foxes use urine to mark their territories. A male fox raises a hind leg and his urine is sprayed in front of him; a female fox squats down so the urine is sprayed between the hind legs. Over 12 different urination positions allow them to precisely control the scent mark.

Red foxes have a pair of anal sacs lined by sebaceous glands. For unknown reasons, the gland's secretions are fluorescent in ultraviolet light. The oval-shaped caudal gland reportedly smells of violets.

Missing: Reward

One morning Mr. G woke up without his penis. It was just missing. There was no blood, no struggle. He tried to remember when he'd last seen it. Certainly he'd gone to the bathroom before bed? Yes, the unflushed toilet confirmed.

There was no actual pain, but an intense, throbbing panic. He shook out all the bedsheets, took the pillowcases off the pillows. He checked under piles of clothes and in the laundry and the shower. He looked in the butter dish.

Finally he had no choice but to get dressed for work. Once there, he contacted anyone who might have seen it, including a handful of old girlfriends. Most of them responded sympathetically, said they'd keep an eye out for it. He left work early, said he wasn't feeling well. At home he tried to eat, watch a movie, listen to music, shower, work out, go for a run, do laundry, call a friend, reread the news... He checked the Craigslist classifieds hourly until finally:

Found: Man's Penis. Please contact me with description.

He called the number. I think you might have my penis, he said.

Can you describe it for me?

Well, it's um, white, well, you know, Caucasian, and um, circumcised, leans slightly to the, um, left...

She gave him an address. The entire drive he panicked—what if it was broken, or ruined? What if it wasn't his? He arrived at her front porch and knocked. The woman opened the door and his face burned. She brought it out, wrapped in a dishtowel. Yes, that's it! he said, relieved. Where did you find it?

It was out by the mailboxes. I didn't touch it, she reassured, turning scarlet.

The Slave

She does whatever you want?

Basically.

But it's not a sexual thing?

Not really. She just wants to be a slave.

That is so fucked up.

My friend's slave was returning from the bathroom, chewing her fingernails.

I'll prove it, he whispered. Hey darlin', get us some water, will ya?

That doesn't prove anything I whispered—I'd get you water.

He rolled his eyes. Wait, he said, before you go, I want you to sit on my friend's lap and stick your tongue in his ear.

She looked at me without smiling. She had on dark jeans, a black t-shirt, straight blond hair one day too greasy, big boobs and big square glasses. Her lipstick was a pale shade of Why Bother. Little bits of a tattoo peeked from her cleavage. She backed one butt cheek onto my knee; her breath smelled biscuity and tannic, her tongue like a moist sponge in my ear.

I waited until she left to wipe my ear dry, and he leaned close. Look, I've got to get rid of her, he whispered. What do you think of her?

I don't want a slave, I said, ordering another beer.

Nobody ever *thinks* they want a slave. But when a girl comes up and says she wants to be your slave, you have to say yes.

Well it's not like I have money to buy a slave.

Look, what I really need right now is a bag of weed. You get me a bag of weed, she's yours.

She returned with the waters and set them down.

Hey look, darlin', I've got to get going, he said, standing up. My friend here is going to take you home, okay?

Call me later, he said, winking and throwing a few bucks on the table.

The Copulatory Tie

Red fox (*vulpes vulpes*) reproduction occurs from January to March when the fox-dog mates with the female vixen. During copulation the bulbus glandis at the base of the penis swells and the sex organs of both male and female become locked together. When the male turns to leave, he cannot.

This "copulatory tie" may last for more than an hour. Couples face away from one another, still joined by their sexual organs. Virgin foxes can become particularly distressed. Some foxes appear to become bored or uncomfortable and one will try to walk away, pulling the other with it. Towards the latter part of their time connected, they are often seen snapping at each other.

Moonlighting

He started acting strange. He started coming home late. He started wearing ties. When he stayed out for an entire Sunday I assumed he was watching the game, but he returned smelling of perfume and went straight to the shower.

I sat on the toilet while he trimmed and then shaved off his beard. What prompted this?

Just trying something new, he said. And spent the night on the couch.

On the third Sunday in a row, I accidentally on purpose stuck my hand in his laundry pocket and found breath mints and a receipt from Macy's.

He was late for dinner again and flushed.

What's going on? I finally said, holding out the receipt. You spent $200 on a new suit?

I have to go to a convention.

You're a mechanic! Are you having an affair?

He denied it.

But it got worse—after the convention he refused to pose for our Christmas card, stopped having sex completely, and moved permanently into the guest room. I broke into his briefcase expecting love letters but found only junk pamphlets and uninteresting receipts.

Finally one Sunday I trailed his Jeep Cherokee across town and into a nice residential neighborhood. He parked and got out in front of a big fancy house with a 3-car garage. I'd never seen him wearing that suit before.

He rang the doorbell. A woman answered. They talked through the screen for a few minutes. Finally she shook her head and closed the door. My husband tucked something into the crack of the screen and left. When he was gone I snuck up to the door. *The Watchtower*, it said.

Jonah

After being swallowed by and then spending three days and three nights in the belly of a whale, Jonah was spit up on the sandy beach, bleached white from digestive juices and speaking a sort of inspired nonsense.

At least you could become a poet, we tried to console.

Ruby Tuesdays

Every franchise has stories: a busy Mother's Day, a dining room full of families eating meatloaf and baked potatoes, the kitchen humming like a beehive and then: Bam! Pirates.

I was rolling silverware on the patio at the end of my shift when I saw the ship with the ragged sails. I was used to seeing ships come into the harbor but this one was different right away, shooting off cannons at all the yachts. Oh shit, my GM said, close the blinds! The last time they were here they shoved shrimp scaloppini down the toilets and stole all the liquor. I won't even tell you how we had to disinfect the salad bar.

But it was too late: we'd already been spotted. The ship turned ever so slightly in our direction and I could see the Jolly Roger.

I can stay late I offered.

But you're already cut he said, you'd have to clock back in.

That's okay I said.

We gathered potential weapons: steak knives, corkscrews, the emergency fire extinguisher from the men's room. Pirates were hanging off the sides, shouting and shooting off pistols.

They exploded through the front door of Ruby Tuesdays. The hostess sat them in my section as the other diners got underneath the tables. A kid started crying and was hushed by its mother. I felt my manager standing behind me as I filled their water cups. Tell them about the specials, he said in a steady voice.

I told them about the soup of the day and the spicy Cajun pasta, I told them there was an additional charge for splitting checks and I had to add gratuity on parties over 6. But they were eyeballing the bar, the kitchen, the cash register, the gold ring on my finger. One of the pirates was already carving his name into the upholstery.

They blew past the GM guarding the register *we don't want any trouble*, and emerged from the kitchen carrying econo-sized jars of mayonnaise, packages of ground beef, blocks of cheese, slabs of bacon, potatoes, and Monday night's special baby back ribs, still marinating in Ruby Tuesdays' signature sauce. Others were stuffing cash and rolls of toilet paper into black garbage bags.

An arm encircled my neck and squeezed; the musky, unwashed smell filled my nostrils. I made eye contact with the GM, tied to the hostess station, as I was dragged outside, the maroon and gold Ruby Tuesdays' sign receding in the distance.

Gekkering

There are over 28 different fox **vocalizations** including:
- barking
- fox distress call
- vixen scream
- alarm bark
- short fox yip
- gekkering
- fox kits playing
- sad red fox kit
- purring
- beautiful howl-like crying
- yelping from a distance
- bark and scream
- strange haunting sound with birds
- young fox crying
- lone fox calling for a mate

My Boyfriend Lives
in an Old Folks Home

Which explains why he wouldn't have me over to his apartment for almost a year. As I was breaking up with him he came clean: I live in an old folks home.

He insists it wasn't always an old folks home, it was just a regular apartment building when I moved in he said, holding open the front glass doors. But when they decided to convert it, I just stayed. I hate moving, he explained. Besides, it's so peaceful and quiet after 9 pm.

There were a cluster of ladies in chairs by the front door wearing their best sweaters, watching us. The fake fire burned in the empty living room. No one ever uses the pool tables he whispered, pulling me down the hallway.

The doorways were covered with macramé wreaths and laminated puzzles and the week's menu printed on colored paper. Isn't it weird? I finally asked as we passed the empty indoor pool and handwritten signs for Bridge Team and Movie Night on Friday.

I mean, sometimes one of the residents has an accident in the elevator and it takes a few days for the smell to leave, he said, and it's always sad when one of them dies...

But they haven't raised my rent in ten years and the workout facilities are practically new, he added, shaking it off.

Crepuscular

The red fox is **crepuscular**, meaning active at dusk. Due to human encroachment on fox territory, foxes are widely regarded as vermin. Most common causes of death include shooting, trapping, road accidents, and secondary poisoning. In Britain foxes are hunted with hounds for sport.

Foxes are listed of "least concern" on the scale of impending extinction threats along with the barn owl, the pigeon, the Madagascar hissing cockroach and the velvet belly lanternshark.

I Met My 20-Year-Old Self in the Lounge Car of the Amtrak

Do you feel old now? she asked.
 I shrugged. Do you feel young?
 We shared a soda as the Midwest rolled by.

The Stewardess

Can I get you anything? my wife asks, handing me a tiny bag of peanuts. She's wearing silver go-go boots and a little neck scarf. The shrink said acting out our fantasies was healthy, so several times a day she shows me how to buckle and unbuckle my safety belt and points out all the emergency exits in the house. She pours me complimentary sodas into small glasses with square ice cubes and hands me expired magazines and tiny pillows.

Sometimes my wife complains about being on her feet all day, and I'll admit I long for extra legroom, but it's a lot better than before, fighting about coffee we don't have and who's turn it was to bury the cat. And even though tipping her is forbidden, sometimes I do anyway, and sometimes she saves me a blanket or doesn't charge me for my headphones. We're going to be okay, I think, when she asks me to please return my tray to the upright position and slips me extra peanuts, it's these little things that tell me we're going to make it.

My Boyfriend Lives in the Tree in Front of My House

And sometimes I bring him Cheetos or popsicles or trashy gossip magazines and sometimes I crawl up there on the lower branches and we let our legs dangle, have a treebranch cocktail, make fun of the guy walking the Chihuahuas or the Vietnam vet on the corner with his platoon of American flags, and then I go home, which is just a few steps away. We see each other on Friday evenings and every other Sunday, because life is complicated after all.

It started before he was my boyfriend, when he hid in the tree to "see the look on my face" when I discovered the present he'd left on my front porch. It was an admittedly lovely tree, and moving in seemed the next logical step. Some nights he sleeps with me in my bed, and some nights we retire to our own spaces, me to my room and him to his tree branch. We've talked about building something more permanent, even a few 2 x 4s for him to properly sit on, but haven't, yet. On the nights we're Not Supposed To See Each Other, he'll sometimes text me anyway and I'll run out with smuggled tacos from dinner and we'll meet on the grass and eat by the light of the lampposts that automatically turn on at 6 pm each night.

Most of the time I commend myself on how great we are about everything, taking space, not rushing in too fast—because lord knows we've both had our share, and we agree that love should be approached like a cobra.

But there's one thing my boyfriend in a tree doesn't know: Sometimes when I'm supposed to be in bed, I stand at the darkened front window and watch the tiny light from his keychain moving behind all the foliage, and I secretly wish he would just climb down and come inside.

The Alpha Male

Confrontations between **alpha male** foxes occur, particularly during mating season. When afraid, red foxes grin in submission, curving their bodies and lashing their tails back and forth. When launching an attack, red foxes approach directly, trying to intimidate. During this "foxtrot" they stand on their hind legs, putting their front paws on each other's upper body and using open-mouthed threats.

What Happened in the Library

Discouraged by the shelves of unread books in my extensive personal library, I made a phone call. The clone I ordered showed up at my doorstep carrying an old red Samsonite hardshell suitcase. Did you bring reading glasses? I asked. She nodded. I showed her to my library. This will be your room, I said. I put a cot out for you, but I don't expect you'll be sleeping much. I also put the armchair and my favorite lamp next to the fireplace.

But it's 100 degrees out, my clone objected.

I knew you would say that, I said, so I also strung up a hammock in the backyard. And eventually summer will be over and you'll want to read by the fireplace.

I walked my clone over to the bookshelves. You can go in any order, maybe Homer, Ovid, Chaucer, Shakespeare, all the way up to Fitzgerald and Hemingway, or you could go alphabetically instead. Drink all the coffee you want. You'll get every other Sunday off.

What if it's raining?

Well, if it's raining on a Sunday then obviously I'm going to need you to stay here and read all day, so if the rainy day happens to fall on a Sunday, you'll get Monday off instead.

I let my clone settle in and I commended myself on my own brilliance.

The first few weeks I was so happy to peek in and find her curled in the armchair, fuzzy socked feet, glass of iced tea, and the crinkly sound of pages turning. Her profile, my own but less tired.

I lugged my lecture notes to and from the university, graded piles of essays. My clone, on the other hand, spent whole days wearing the same nightgown, or reading in the nude on the hammock wearing a cowboy hat. When I saw *Moby Dick* propped on her brown belly as I left to catch the Lightrail, I felt a true pang of jealousy.

I decided to spy on her. With all this time to read, she really should have finished more books. I pretended to leave one day but secretly cancelled all my classes and drove to the nearby Office Max where I took a cab home and hid in the bushes below my front window. My clone was just waking up, *Moby Dick* opened beside her on the bed. She had been reading that same book for quite some time now—months, even. She sat and stretched, turned on the reading light, reached for the chocolate croissant I'd left her, pulled her red Samsonite suitcase from under the bed, and retrieved a book I hadn't seen before. She settled into the pillows, croissant in one hand and the book, opened to the middle, in the other, and I could finally read the title: *50 Shades of Gray*.

On the next non-rainy Sunday when my clone had the day off I broke into her red Samsonite suitcase and found books with titles like: *The Vampire's Last Kiss, Erotic Exchanges, The Mistress' Club*, and *Lust on the Amazon*. I opened the beautiful hardbound edition of *Moby Dick* she'd been reading for months and found it gutted, a copy of *A Girl's Guide to Getting a Husband* neatly tucked inside.

What is going on here? I asked her when she returned Monday morning.

What are you talking about?

How's *Moby Dick*?

It's good.

What's happening?

Well, they're chasing around this whale and stuff.

And?

Um, they're talking a lot about whales and stuff.

And?

I don't know! *Moby Dick* sucks, okay! I hate it!

Her face blanched, but it was too late.

I contacted the cloning agency and had her returned. I turned down their offer of a replacement—it was still too soon. But the library seemed so empty, I thought, cleaning up her crumbs, putting her cowboy hat on the shelf.

True Tales From Therapy #5

Though there was absolutely no correlation between seeing a new therapist, and that therapist killing himself with a shotgun the following week, Mr. G couldn't help wonder, for just a fleeting second, if his wife's claim that *everyone was sick of listening to him whine about his problems* had some validity.

The Fox and the Salamander

In the Achomawi creation myth, Fox and Coyote are the co-creators of the world, who leave just before the arrival of humans.

The Yurok tribe believed that Fox captured the sun and tied him to a hill, causing him to burn a great hole in the ground.

In Japanese mythology, the kitsune are fox-like spirits possessing magical abilities, including the ability to assume human form.

An Inuit story tells of how Fox, in the guise of a beautiful woman, tricks a hunter into marrying her, only to resume her true form after he offends her.

In Arab folklore, the fox is said to feign death by filling its abdomen with air in order to appear bloated and wait for prey.

In Greek mythology, the Cadmean vixen was a gigantic fox destined never to be caught.

In the Cotswolds, witches were thought to take the shape of foxes in order to steal butter from their neighbors.

The authors of the Bible applied the word "fox" to false prophets (Ezekiel 13:4) and the hypocrisy of Herod Antipas (Luke 13:32).

Lot's Wife

"Don't look back!" the angel yelled while the sky above Sodom and Gomorrah rained fire. "For god's sake don't look at it!"

They ran across the sizzling desert, beating their heads, burying their faces, throwing sand in their eyes. Lot's wife tried to ignore the screams of people burning, the filtered light of sun and smoke at her back.

As they crested Mount Sodom she paused for just one moment and turned around.

It was even better than she had imagined, an exotic abyss that swallowed her retinas and lifted her onto a heroin cloud of transgression. As her eyes burned up, and her skin stiffened into salt, the last thing she remembered was a conversation she'd had with Eve, naked, beautiful Eve making apple fritters, her lips still stained. *It was beautiful* she'd confessed.

Fox V: The Adulterer

Foxes in your hen house? Get a Pederick Leg Hold Fox Trap with 1 ½ coilspring double jaw trap. Heavy duty spring wire. For Fox, Fisher, Marten, Mink, Muskrat, Nutria, Opossum, Raccoon, Skunk and Woodchuck. Made and assembled in the USA!

I have a fox problem, the boyfriend said, showing the newspaper ad.

Yea, the wife's poodle got eaten by one last year right around this time. They feel the cold coming and it makes them nuts, he says. Your wife send you down here?

My fiancée, he said, which was a lie because of course she had no idea.

You want to trap it or kill it?

I just want it to go away.

Well, if you trap it and let it go, it's coming back. And when it comes back, it knows you're a sucker.

He looked over the assortment of guns, camouflage, mess kits, and ground pads. The man behind the counter took all the information; he was wearing a shirt that read Elf: The Other White Meat. Should come by the end of the week, he said. Hopefully you can manage that long.

When the boyfriend left the store it was already getting dark. The trap was jangling inside the box, some assembly required. And for a minute he felt bad, driving past Jackass Hill and a blinding sunset...and then he started to get pissed again.

He was speeding, and that's when the bastard went running across the street. Maybe it was the smug expression, the smarmy way he slinked in front of the car, but instinctively the leg went heavy on the gas pedal and his little face and stupid bushy tail came hurtling forward. The boyfriend heard a slight thud and a mewing scream like a weird baby as the fox limped into someone's back yard.

Isaac's Father

One day Isaac's sweet, doting father took him for a walk in the desert. He was acting strange. He was carrying rope.

Where are we going, Father?

You'll see.

They kept walking and walking, away from everyone, until they reached the mountaintop. The view was washed with pinks and yellows like an overexposed photograph. Isaac's father grabbed him, kissed his forehead, and then squeezed him tight—too tight—then forced him face down onto a flat slab of stone and tied him with rope.

Father, what are you doing?! But the ropes were tight and the valley was empty.

Isaac's father pulled out a giant butchering knife, the one used to slaughter goats, and held it up, poised.

God made me do it, he sobbed.

The Magician's Assistant

All those nights of illusion it was bound to happen—a slip of the knife and the trick would be for real. I was halved like a papaya, right through my torso and between the hemispheres of my brain—my beauty mark went one way, my cowlick went the other.

They covered it well, the audience didn't know. My body went into shock as the assistants carried the two halves of me into the wings.

Oh shit! I'm so sorry! the magician sobbed backstage, covering his face.

It's okay, we knew someday this might happen I said as they fired up the soldering guns. I looked away from the other half of me wincing, the curl of smoke rising between us as they tried and failed to reconnect us.

Brunch

Last Sunday we all went to brunch at Waffle House like we do every Sunday after church except this Sunday I was dead.

I sat there stiff but my friends didn't seem to care, asking about my Eggs Benedict, commenting on my new dress. I couldn't hold my fork, rigor mortis already setting in, and one of them jellied my toast and lifted my mimosa to my lips. When the waiter returned my plate was cold and untouched; he refilled our water glasses and my friends kindly had my food boxed up for me and even split the tab in a way that I didn't have to chip in, which was nice since I didn't have a wallet anymore.

She's dead one of them explained as the waiter brought the to-go box.

I Found Your Voodoo Doll on the Dance Floor After Last Call

It was squishy under my feet and at first I thought it was a wad of napkins. But as the crowds cleared, it became obvious. It looked just like me if I'd been made out of cornstalks and had button eyes. *Is that really how you see me?* I thought as I picked it up and smoothed the yarn hair.

My first instinct was to toss it into the dumpster but I had doubts—what if it landed on its head? Was stabbed by sharp cardboard? What if I woke in the morning and found myself buried alive or impaled on a U-Haul box?

The mantle was out of the question, too far to fall if the cat knocked it down. A cabinet wouldn't work—there was suffocation, asphyxiation. Anything near a sink was out. Nothing near the fireplace, on the balcony, near a window.

A bird cage seemed the best solution.

One day I rushed home from work and the cage door was open, the voodoo doll missing. I stared a blank, button-eyed stare into its empty depths.

When I saw you at the bar later, voodoo doll on a chain around your neck, I collapsed to my knees in front of you. Thank god, I said.

I knew you'd be back, you said.

The Lightrail

I knew everything would change but I didn't expect it to happen so quickly. Ever since I was a child I'd imagined what it would be like. We weren't poor, but the Lightrail was almost 30 minutes away and by the time we got there it was standing room only, a sea of raised arms and armpits. I was taught to look politely away from those who lived close, sitting down comfortably, lipstick and hair perfect.

When I signed the lease even my dad was impressed. He stood with my mom in the empty apartment, opened and closed drawers, looked in all the closets, and then asked me to take a picture of him which he later sent to all his friends: *My daughter's new apartment, just 100 feet from the Lightrail. Her mother and I are so proud.*

News of my housewarming party spread fast; my apartment was full of bodies and faces I hadn't thought about in years. "Yeah," one said, "I wasn't going to come but then I heard you lived next to the Lightrail." The next morning people were still there, drinking coffee and watching *The Price is Right,* something that never happened when I lived above Bath and Body Works.

Pretty soon my best friend stopped returning my calls. "Well, I just figured you're too busy to call now that you live next to the Lightrail," she said. Over the coming weeks the phone stayed silent, the neighbors waved from a respectful distance, even the postman called me Ma'am when he handed me junk mail for credit cards with higher limits.

I found myself purposely missing my stop in the evenings, riding past the lit up Walgreens, past the bar and grill where I once got food poisoning. For two days I just watched everything go by: the abandoned rubber factory with the broken windows and the elaborate graffiti, the junkyard full of retired Lightrail cars, the hole by the tracks where I once saw a baby fox.

Finally I had to go home. When I got there the apartment was dark and barren and I locked the door and pulled the shades and sat under the window while the *ding ding* of the Lightrail sounded like an unholy lullaby.

The River

Our story was poisoning me and I had to get rid of it. So I put it in a pillowcase and dragged it to the river. It was beating against the bag like a man sentenced to die, and I kept a firm grip on it even though my fingers were cold. When I got to the bank I paused only one moment before I submerged it, held it down until it stopped twitching and the bag filled with river water and I watched it float away.

Eve

Don't you want more than this? the snake asked, sliding around her bicep.

I never thought about it.

You've never thought about more than fruit trees? There's New York, Hollywood, champagne, yachts, drugs that make you feel amazing. Here, try this.

The apple was perfect and red. The orgasm lasted for hours. When she awoke she was naked and Adam was missing a rib.

Art Installation: Exhibit #2558

You Twisted My Spite Into Sculpture—1997
United States
Mixed media: garbage bags, plaster of Paris, broken
jewelry, straws, boyfriend
On permanent loan from the artist
Artist Statement: *Mask making has always held a special place in my work. I believe there is an inherent fear of asphyxiation present in the creative relationship. This piece began as a mask but I soon realized a simple mask no longer was able to encompass the plight of current society—today's citizen wants love but feels trapped. My work explores the implications of falsifying our true nature. The piece is really about transforming everyday negativity into art.*

The crowd clustered around the sculpture, the crude plaster, the bits of broken jewelry cemented into the patina. The figure stood almost defiantly, two straws poking from the nostrils and the only movement a sort of desperate darting of the eyeballs.

Samson

"Don't worry, we'll both do it," Delilah said, reaching for the hair clippers on the counter next to the lice shampoo.

#86 Manny Williams

Last Saturday I went to the grocery store for chicken and noodles and there in aisle 5 was a life-sized cardboard cutout of Denver wide receiver Manny Williams. He was holding a pitcher of lemonade and had the words 'Hydrate naturally!' written across his chest. Since my husband's a Broncos fan, I took a picture of myself kissing Manny Williams and sent it to him for fun.

I didn't get any response and so over dinner I just came right out and asked: What did you think of my picture?

Cute he said gruffly. He slept with his back to me that night and left in the morning without saying goodbye.

The next day when I got home the Manny Williams cardboard cutout was waiting in the living room with a note: They were going to throw it out. He has a bit of a horse face, don't you think?

Manny's smile was frozen in place, his hair tousled and wet, black smudges under his eyes, lemonade in his hands. He was cute I conceded, but nothing to make such a fuss over.

It was odd having a life-sized Manny Williams smiling from the corner of my living room, but I hadn't thought of a better place to move him by the time my husband came home. Did you two have a nice day? he asked, not making eye contact.

That night I slept badly on the couch, but the warm orange light of the fireplace flickered off Manny's eyes in a way that felt oddly comforting.

When I woke my husband had already left. I looked over at Manny and saw the words 'I Have a Small Penis' scrawled across his chest where 'Hydrate naturally!' used to be. I took the whole day off work to scrub him free.

The next day was Sunday. Aren't you watching the game I asked?

My husband stared at me without speaking, then said—how can you even ask me that?

He hadn't come home by supper when I received a picture of him next to a cardboard cutout of Miss America. I won't be home tonight, his message said.

All night I cried, and Manny comforted me with his unwavering smile. Thanks for listening I said, scooting closer and throwing an edge of the afghan over his legs.

The Introduction

They'd been dating long enough that it was time. He warned her that it might take a while to warm up, so not to take it personally. She promised she wouldn't. On the chosen day she spent an hour deciding what to wear— nothing too old, too young, too overbearing, or like she was trying too hard. They all met for ice cream on neutral territory. Nice to meet you, she said, on her best behavior, extending her hand, but the penis gave her only a limp return handshake. Ice cream was tense, as the penis slumped in the booth and refused to eat. Just give him some time, the boyfriend reassured. He's probably a little jealous.

So they took it slow, picnics in the park, trips to the zoo, the penis would sulk but then light up at the boa constrictor cage. She always came armed with gift cards to Subway and new headphones and donuts and bottles of Orangina.

The first time she spent the night the penis kept them both up all night, coughing and complaining of non-existent stomachaches and needing multiple glasses of water. Thanks for being so understanding, the boyfriend said as the penis finally nodded off. Once he gets to know you he will love you.

But in the bathroom she found the contents of her purse scattered, the hairbrush handle snapped. The stairs were booby trapped with jelly beans.

Look, she finally said, sitting her boyfriend down—
we have to talk about your penis. I'm trying everything,
but it's just not working. He resents me being here.

As they were talking, the penis came in and changed
the channel to porn. What are you doing? the boyfriend
yelled.

What? We always watch this.

That's it, the boyfriend said, dragging the penis into
the other room. She could hear the muffled yelling:
Don't ruin this for me!

There was crashing in the kitchen as the penis, mid-
tantrum, began to knock things over. She turned off the
television, collected her belongings and let herself out.

The Private Investigator

I walked into his office and closed the door. There were piles of papers everywhere and an inflatable moose head hanging on the wall.

What can I do for you? he asked.

Well, I just don't know what I'm doing half the time, I said. I think it would be great if you could keep an eye on me.

Sure, he said. Is someone threatening you?

No, nothing like that. It's just me. I can't trust myself anymore.

Any clues or suspicions?

No...but the whole thing is pretty suspicious.

He pats my hand. You've done the right thing, he says. Usually if you suspect something to be true, it is.

I left his office feeling much better. Almost immediately the eyes were upon me—cars that followed a bit too close and too long, people watching me from across the street. At home a red light blinked between the books on my bookshelf.

A week later I returned to his office. Well, we have news to report, he said. Are you ready?

Yes, I nodded, sitting down.

The first picture was my car parked in front of the post office. If you'll notice, he said, circling areas of the photo, this is a no-parking zone and the sign is clearly displayed. Subject arrived at 3:14pm and parked for 23 minutes, in blatant violation.

I nodded, didn't say anything as he handed me the photo.

During the car ride home, subject picked her nose and then, after looking around, consumed it. At 5:17 subject arrived home, drew all the blinds, and proceeded to watch xxx-rated videos for 17 minutes, the final one, *80-year-old grandpa does his nurse*, commencing at 5:34.

After watching video, subject stared at the computer for 1 hour and 46 minutes without pants on. The phone rang on three different occasions and subject ignored calls.

Subject smoked marijuana at 9:16 and then took a bath while drinking an airplane-sized bottle of cinnamon flavored whiskey. During bath, subject appeared to have a conversation with no one that lasted 11 minutes.

At 11:34, subject got into bed and read *To Kill A Mockingbird* until 12:13, when she turned off the lamp to presumably sleep. Then most curious of all: at 12:21, just 8 minutes later, subject got out of bed and laid directly in the middle of a moonbeam shining through the skylight. Subject cried until 12:31.

He handed the stack of pictures to me. After that, our man couldn't see anything else.

I sighed. I'm not completely surprised.

If it makes you feel any better, I see this kind of thing all the time.

I guess it's better to know for sure.

I'm sorry to be the one to have to tell you, he added, handing me a tissue.

Fox VI: The Vixen Scream

Daylight was thin, fatigued with cold. I'd wake in time to see an anorexic sun slip behind dirty clouds. Piles of snow lay abandoned like cold mashed potatoes. My breath condensed on the window plastic. It had been months since I'd last seen him, but I thought of him often as I huddled by the fireplace, drank cherry brandy in the candy-colored lights while icicles dripped. Sometimes I left food out, pans of enchiladas or holiday fruitcakes, but they were mostly untouched, even by the squirrels.

So I was surprised the night I heard gekkering outside my bedroom window. In the moonlight I only saw moving shadows, and it wasn't until they separated that I recognized him, scruffy in a new winter coat, locked in battle with a coyote. They were poised with teeth bared, snouts wrinkled. My fox looked vicious in a way I'd never seen before.

I got dressed and put on my warmest coat. When I emerged into the bluish light there was a mess of snow where they'd quarreled and blood leading under the bushes, a quiet whimpering. You're hurt, I said. I knelt in front of the bush. He seemed like he wanted to come out but couldn't. Trust me, I cooed. I got on all fours and crawled behind the hedge, onto the packed snow where the moonlight was strange and mottled. His entire backside and beautiful tail was covered in blood, the left leg oddly twisted. I took off my glove and touched as lightly as I could but when I tried to move it he growled and nipped at my fingers, not enough to hurt me but enough.

Oh love, I said, pressing my cheek to his face while my world went watery. I didn't hear the creak of the metal hinges or the release of the spring until the teeth of the foxtrap clamped deeply into my thigh.

The Tower of Babel

They say that Nimrod, the great-grandson of Noah, was still haunted by the Great Flood when he built Babel—haunted by forty days of floating, the stench of confused animals, and endless rains drowning the earth until they were the only ones left.

Each day in Babylon the tower stretched higher. The crowds fired bricks and mortar, feeding the growing stalagmite that would eventually breach the heavens and allow them to demand answers.

But God was displeased and unleashed the confusion of tongues, 72 languages where there had only been one. Dumbfounded, they stopped building and shouted words that none could decipher. Untranslated sadness spilled from their lips, and they watched friends and lovers fall away in a manner that no one could have anticipated.

The Genie

The genie was trapped inside a pink glass perfume bottle, square panels distorting her face. When I opened the bottle she materialized in hissing pink steam.

Do I get three wishes? I asked.

I suppose, she said. Or what about a violin sonata? I know everything by Debussy.

I'd rather just have the wishes I said. How about $1,000,000?

That's so cliché, she said.

Okay, then how about my mortgage is paid?

Done she said, and shrunk back into her pink bottle.

It was amazing the quiet that ensued once the phone wasn't ringing all the time. When I came home from work she was painting bars on her bottle.

I have another wish I said. I'd like my house to be on the coast of Barcelona overlooking the water.

Done she said. And then we were sitting on a window ledge watching the blue crashing waters of Costa Brava.

We sat listening and watching.

After your third wish I'm free, you know, she said.

I just need a little more time, I said.

Maybe I was being an asshole. Maybe I was just lonely. But when I could put it off no longer I said—Ok. I'd like to be 20 years younger but still have all my current intelligence.

Are you sure, she said? It's so much easier not to know.

Yes, I said.

Done she said. And in the confusion I didn't notice what had happened until I was inside the bottle looking through the square panels into a distorted pink world.

The Diaspora

Maybe I should have known when you were resisting Paris with such vigor. You'd talked of nothing else for years, yet you flinched when I presented you with the tickets. You knew. Maybe you thought you could beat it. That should have been my first clue.

Or I could have done the math and realized that your proud Parisian family was completely displaced: one in Peru, one in Scotland, one in South Africa, you in America and three in Argentina, not counting Raquel herself, so desperate for Paris in her empty home in Buenos Aires that even the maid had to speak French.

But my first clue came under the Eiffel Tower of all places, symbol of romantic Paris. You were pacing. Cursing in French. Already a bad sign. Our first full day there. Still jetlagged. I guess you'd been gone too long, forgot why the rest of your family moved away, and I didn't put it all together until I saw your fangs.

The Golden Calf

At first the people said things like *all is as it should be* and *God will take care of us* and stuff like that. But Moses was gone for a long time. They thought he'd be back in a few days. Then a week. Then a month. Hope followed disappointment followed hope until their faith began to shrivel. Sure the manna was there today but what about *tomorrow*?

By the time the calf was underway no one really knew whose idea it had been. Create something to focus on, stave off the fear. It seemed a small thing to remove a ring, an earring, to toss some charm from the old country, a lone idol snuck under a shawl. And it was beautiful, it really was. The smell of molten gold, the way the people laughed.

Bats: A Love Story

The Mexican Free-Tailed Bat migrates each year from the caves of Carlsbad to the abandoned Orient Mine in the Sangre de Cristo Mountains. The new generation has never seen the Orient Mine but they fly anyway, following some great calling they do not question. Every summer evening, when the pink ball of sun finally disappears behind mountain silhouettes, the bats awaken and exit the mine in what we've been told is a spectacular exodus.

And so we wait, hands stuffed in pockets, whispering. We almost changed our minds. We're still at the beginning, of course. This is our first hike, our first trip...mud and darkness and whether the bat spectacle is exaggerated—these are the things that will determine our relationship.

When it's almost too dark to see the first one appears, a lone bat flying erratically toward the receding sun. Then another. One by one the cloud thickens, a dark waterfall pouring from the mouth of the cave and cascading to the valley floor. The bats hurl their screams into the dark, wait for the answers to bounce back and show them the way,

We stand silenced with recognition under the holy cloud of 150,000 suede wings. We, too, know what it means to cry out blindly in great silences. My hands crawl under your coat for warmth.

Turtle Tears

When a female leatherback turtle hauls her 1500-pound body onto the dark sands of Zoni Beach, digs a hole with her fins, and lays a bunch of squishy, ping pong ball-sized eggs, she's often seen crying. But the thickened tears that slip from her eyes during this hour of nesting are just vehicles for salt, the leatherback's way of purging her body. So even though it looks like crying, it's just detoxing.

Yes, but you're not a turtle, he reminds me, handing me a tissue.

Fox VII: The End

If I'd found his whole body it would have been over, but I found only his tail.

I belted it to myself to keep it safe, and pretty soon it became part of me without the belt. I could feel it lightly brushing the backs of my legs when I walked. And even though it looked funny, and even though I had to cut holes in all my skirts, it did feel more honest.

They say if a fox loses its tail it will grow a new one, but the last time I saw him it hadn't grown back. He was on the bike path behind the Lightrail where we'd first met, a funny compensated balance in his gait. He pretended not to see me. I sat on my haunches beside him and flicked the tail, not to flaunt but just to show it was safe. We sat in the sun and shared a mouse in silence.

Requiem *for piano*

She'd been slipping away from him slowly, as the things that hurt most do. He woke one morning and nuzzled his arm into the swooping curve of her waist only to find it cold, with a hardened glossy varnish that could only mean to keep him out. He tried to fit his body into the new curve but it was stiff and unforgiving.

Her long ballerina arms and legs were next. They, too, hardened and reached for the floor, anchoring her growing weight until she became too heavy to move. Her ribs cracked open and widened into a wooden soundboard, the strands of her long curly hair stiffened and elongated until he could no longer run his fingers through them. Pulled taut, they vibrated and wept if touched, crying the last of the unshed tears that now landed like dampened hammers on strings.

It was happening but he couldn't stop it, could only awaken each morning to what remained of his beloved and take frightened inventory: her toes reduced to golden pedals, her polished satin black skin, her long spine a lacquered lid that reflected his bewilderment.

Her face went last. On that final morning her smile stretched into 88 white ivories, feathered with the sharps and flats of dark lashes. In the soft morning light he played a requiem on her still-warm keys, propping the lid to listen to her heart.

Exodus

I wanted to keep walking and pretend I hadn't seen it. I knew plenty about bags floating in rivers. It wiggled, and I knew I should stop but I didn't, and I was reminded of my mother sneaking me down to the edge of the river, showing me all the empty bags left in the mud like used condoms—look at those stories, she would say, people just threw them away like trash! They could have lived. And then she would fall to her knees and pray to her god.

I saw the woman leaving the edge of the river. I avoided eye contact with all the gypsies, beating deflated pillowcases against rocks as I crawled up the muddy banks and caught the tail of the story. I dragged the waterlogged thing out and took it home, where I set its cold, blue body gently on the page and let it live.

January Sky

Geese congregated on the frozen lake, rabbits hid in the bare bushes, field mice huddled in the brown dead grass. There was a soft, fated quality in the air. I was thinking about the past—that barefoot summer, a den by the train tracks, the smell of musk and dirt, the way the sun hung on late into the night...when I stopped.

The coyote was just a few feet ahead of me on the sidewalk, pouncing into the bare bushes. He glanced at me and then resumed walking. He was bigger than a fox. I kept a safe distance behind him. His hips had a confident swagger. I followed him as the cacophony of geese faded.

We walked single file around the lake, inhaling the unmistakable smell of life poised and ready—fish stirring under the ice, green bulbs awakening below the ground. Soon the water would be free, the leaves would unfold like handkerchiefs, the flowers swell with pollen, the butterflies return. The risks of spring were still trapped under the ice but one good thaw and they would be released.

The coyote sniffed the wind and held my gaze. Greenish eyes that didn't look away.

Thanks

My deepest thanks to Nick Busheff, Kona Morris, and Sally Reno for their amazing insights, guidance and encouragement through the many drafts of this manuscript, as well as David Wagner, Bryan Jansing, E.B. Giles, Laura Keenan, Leah Rogin-Roper, Jonathan Montgomery, Nicholas Morris, and Meg Tuite.

I'm also indebted to my years with Fast Forward Press as well as to everyone currently involved in The FBomb Reading Series for providing both a catalyst and a venue for me to refine flash fiction.

And finally this book wouldn't exist without Rob Geisen. I'm forever grateful.

Acknowledgments

Several of these stories have been previously published online (sometimes under different titles), and these are: 'Death Row Hugger' in *Boston Literary Magazine*; 'The Fox' in *Santa Fe Literary Review*; 'What Happened in the Library' and 'My House is in the Contemporary Art Museum' in *Connotation Press*; 'My Boyfriend Lives in the Tree in Front of My House' in *Metazen*; 'The Mermaid' and 'The Homunculus' in *Revolver*; 'Exodus' in *Flash Frontier*; 'The Hostess' in *Pure Slush*; 'I Pawned My Boyfriend for $85' in *Blue Five Notebook*; 'Requiem for piano' in *Literary Orphans*; 'I'm Being Stalked by the Avon Lady' in *Cease, Cows*; 'The Private Investigator' in *Atticus Review*; 'The Annunciation' in *Cliterature*; 'True Tales From Therapy #5' in *Right Hand Pointing*; 'Indentured' in *Blink Ink*; 'The Diaspora' in *Zero Ducats*; 'Art Installation: Exhibit #2558' in *Exquisite Duet*.

'Bats: a Love Story' was published in the print anthology *What's Nature Got to Do With It?*, and 'The Detritus' in the print anthology *Flash 101: Surviving the Fiction Apocalypse*.

Information was used from the following webpages:
• http://en.wikipedia.org/wiki/Canidae for 'Canidae';
• http://www.soundboard.com/sb/Fox_Sounds_audio for 'Gekkering';
• http://en.wikipedia.org/wiki/Foxes_in_popular_culture for 'The Fox and the Salamander';

• http://en.wikipedia.org/wiki/Red_fox for 'The Alpha Male', 'The Copulatory Tie', 'Crepuscular' and 'Vulpes Vulpes'.

About the Author

Born on Paradise Island to a race of Amazon warriors, Nancy Stohlman came to America to fight for peace, justice and truth. Her tools include her Lasso of Truth—a rope that compels truth-telling from those bound by it—her bullet-deflecting bracelets, and an invisible plane that flies faster than the speed of sound.

Her books include *The Monster Opera* (2013), *Searching for Suzi: a flash novel* (2009), *Live From Palestine* (2003) and three anthologies of flash fiction including *Fast Forward: The Mix Tape* (2010), which was a finalist for a Colorado Book Award. She is one of the founders of Fast Forward Press, the creator and curator of The FBomb Flash Fiction Reading Series, and the impetus behind Flashnano in November.

By night Nancy straps on stilettos and becomes the lead singer of the lounge metal band Kinky Mink. She dreams of one day becoming a pirate.

Find more about Nancy at www.nancystohlman.com

Other books from *Pure Slush*

Visit the *Pure Slush* Store online:
http://pureslush.webs.com/store.htm

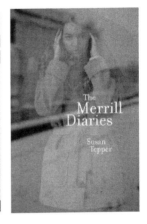

The Company of Men
by Luisa Brenta
ISBN: 978-1-925101-06-5

Many Fish to Fry
by Abha Iyengar
ISBN: 978-1-925101-59-1

The Merrill Diaries
by Susan Tepper
ISBN: 978-0-9922778-2-6

itch
by Gary Percesepe
ISBN: 978-1-925101-21-8

Hard
by Dusty-Anne Rhodes
ISBN: 978-1-925101-80-5

Glass Animals
by Stephen V. Ramey
ISBN: 978-1-925101-86-7